# Disney
## Winnie the Pooh
# A Portrait of
# Friendship

Disney PRESS

**P**iglet painted pictures of everything in the Hundred-Acre
Wood. He painted the tall, leafy trees. And the bright, yellow sun.
And flowers of every size and color.

One day Piglet decided he wanted to paint what he loved best of all in the Wood: his friends!

Piglet asked Pooh and the rest of his friends if they would each sit for a portrait.

"Why, Piglet, I'd be honored!" said Pooh. Everyone else felt the same way.

The next day, Piglet set up his studio outside in the sunshine.

He was ready to begin with Pooh.

Piglet soon saw Pooh heading his way.

"Hello, Pooh," Piglet said. "It is time for your portrait."

Pooh stopped walking. "Oh, is that now?" he asked, a little bewildered. "I thought it was time to fill up my honeypot—and my tummy." Pooh gave his tummy a pat and looked at Piglet.

Pooh didn't want to let down his friend. "All right, Piglet," he said. "You can paint my picture now.

"I'm sure my tummy can wait," he added, though he was not at all certain.

"Now try to sit still, Pooh,"
Piglet said.

Pooh did. But his tummy
did not. It rumbled to the
left and it rumbled to the
right. Finally, Pooh's tummy
rumbled him up onto his feet.

"Sorry, Piglet, but perhaps
now is not a good time to sit still
after all," said Pooh as he picked
up his honeypot and followed his
tummy.

Piglet tried painting Rabbit next. He worked for a few minutes, then gave Rabbit a bunch of carrots to hold.

"These remind me of my garden," said Rabbit, jumping up. "And my garden reminds me that I have work to do. I'm sorry, Piglet, but we'll have to finish another time." Rabbit hurried off.

Tigger had no trouble with Piglet painting his picture. The trouble was all Piglet's, since Tigger couldn't stop bouncing with excitement. "Sorry, Pigalet, but bouncing is what tiggers do best!" Tigger cried.

While Piglet waited for Tigger to stop bouncing,
Kanga and Roo arrived. They were excited to have
their family portrait painted by Piglet.

But Tigger was so excited to see Roo,
he snatched up his little buddy and the
two bounced off into the Wood.

Kanga proved to be good at sitting still for a little while. But before Piglet could finish, she suddenly gasped and jumped up.

"Oh, dear! I must go and take my cupcakes out of the oven," she said.

Piglet had much better luck with Eeyore, who sat as still and as gray as a rock.

"Eeyore, yours is the only portrait I've been able to finish," said Piglet.

"That's too bad," said Eeyore.

"Everyone else had too much to do," said Piglet.

"I'm just doing what I always do, too. Not much," said Eeyore.

Then he lumbered off to do not much somewhere else.

Piglet thought for a moment. "That's it!" he cried. "I need to paint my friends doing what they always do!"

Piglet packed up his art supplies and went to find Pooh. He painted Pooh following a bee.

Then he painted several bees
following Pooh.

Buzzzzzzzzzzzz

Piglet especially liked the painting he did of Pooh finally
getting a smackerel of honey.

Piglet went to Rabbit's garden next. Instead of asking Rabbit to stay still, he stood and painted while his subject moved about in his garden.

He painted several wonderful scenes of Rabbit at work.

At Kanga and Roo's house, Piglet started a new painting, this one with the two of them together.

"Oh, dear," said Piglet. He sniffed his paintbrush. "I believe I've dipped my paintbrush into the icing!"

It turned out to be a very cozy—and yummy—picture.

Piglet couldn't wait to show everyone his portraits.
He invited his friends to view them.

Pooh and the others walked around and looked at
one painting after another. They were very silent,
which was unusual. Piglet began to worry.

Did his friends not like his artwork?

Finally, Pooh cleared his throat. "I'd like to say how wonderful
your paintings are, Piglet." Then he looked thoughtful. "I'd also
like to apologize."

"Whatever for, Pooh?" asked Piglet.

"For saying I'd sit still for you and then, well, not sitting still," said Pooh sheepishly.